ISBN: 9798335216487
Imprint: Independently published

Cover design by: Ryan J. Powell; Myles Murphy
Library of Congress Control Number: 2018675309
Printed in the United States of America

Contents

Trigger Warning

This is a book of **<u>extreme horror</u>**.

Some content may be upsetting.

Reader discretion is advised.

Dollface

R.J. Powell

Chapter One

The pustule on Papa's penis was beginning to itch, but he didn't mind. Each time he came, it helped relieve the pressure behind it.

Squeak.

Squeak.

Squeak.

The rusted bedposts continued to squeak with each pump Papa put

into his newest victim, the pustule rubbing violently against her vaginal walls.

"I can't cum," he groaned as he panted deep into Rebecca's tangled hair. Collapsing on top of her, he slowly pulled his bloodied penis out of her. She began to sob beneath him.

"Can you let me go now?" she asked, nodding toward her wrists tied to the rusty bedposts.

Papa grunted as he moved off her, the bed squeaking furiously beneath his naked weight. His bare feet touched the cool floor of the humid basement, sending a shiver up his spine.

"No," he groaned at her ridiculous request. Rebecca was brand new, having just snatched her up this

afternoon, and he intended to use her to his full advantage.

"I'll be right back," he said before he exited the room and headed up the wooden stairs to his small apartment just above.

The wind and rain continued to howl outside, just as it had when he scooped Rebecca off the highway earlier in the day. He knew that no one would hear her screams with the constant storm outside.

Papa walked to his bedroom, his tiny penis standing erect beneath the fat fold of his hairy stomach.

"There's my girl," he said as he reached for the small doll sitting on the shelf just above his bed. She had tired eyes on a small frame with a pink dress covering her silicone body

Dolly. She looked back at him, her deep-set eyes appearing melancholy. "Give that pussy to Papa. Such a good girl. Such a *good* little girl."

He continued pumping in and out of the human teenager, the blood from Rebecca's hymen mixing with his pre-cum before pulling out completely.

"Dolly, I think she's the one," he groaned. "She's my perfect princess."

With a quick motion, he slid Dollface's floral panties to the side and entered her child-like body.

"Ohh, yes," Papa cried out as he came inside the lifeless doll, cum and blood dripping down her hole as her depth was too shallow to hold all of it. Her plastic curls bounced with each pushing motion into her.

shelf above his bed before collapsing onto the mattress with a thud. It wasn't long before white specks of crust formed at the corner of his mouth, and he was snoring.

∞∞∞

Dollface could feel the blood of the virgin coursing through her silicone canal that still held the remnants of Papa's ejaculate.

"What's happening to me?" she thought to herself. "I have *thoughts*?!"

The blood penetrated every rubber fiber of her being, making its way around her hips, down her legs, up her abdomen, down her arms, and back up again, finding its resting place deep within her mind.

"I can feel..." she thought to herself once more.

The blood continued to course through her skin, giving her cheeks a

flushed hue as it moved to her mouth. Her lip twitched, then slowly began to move.

"I …" she said. "I can… talk."

The blood continued swirling around her face, elevating her silicone beauty. Dollface's pink eyes flicked from side to side before blinking slowly once, then twice, then rapidly. Her brown hair seemed to come alive as the plastic curls gave way to luscious locks of real hair, even with the scent of coconut.

Dollface looked at her hands, examining the fingernails that had miraculously appeared. It was as if she were being born for the first time, just a little later than usual.

Suddenly, flashbacks came to her mind. Papa grunting over

multiple young girls, searching ever-so-diligently for his perfect virgin princess, a life-like version of her, but older. She recalled all the conversations Papa had with himself throughout the years. How he couldn't bring himself to kidnap an actual small child because he didn't want to deal with them, so that's why he always used her. The countless evenings, sometimes going into all hours of the night, with his cock inside her. Stretching her out.

The memories were like a floodgate of emotions and feelings Dollface had never experienced before. One feeling she couldn't quite put her finger on was beginning to stir in the pit of her stomach. She recalled Papa complaining about the same issue once. It was before he went away for a

while. Strange men appeared and took his computer, so Papa wasn't happy, and then he didn't come home for many years.

Dollface sat in silence as she recalled counting dust particles that built up on the tip of her nose during that time.

What was the word Papa used?

She continued to sit with her mind for a few moments before her face lit up.

"Anger," she said aloud, her voice appearing as a squeak.

Dolly was angry. She hated Papa and what he always did to the girls. She knew he was a bad man, and she thought to herself at that moment that she would stop at nothing to seek

her revenge.

Chapter Two

Papa slept hard on the mattress, his oversized stomach folding so far over that you could no longer see his penis. The mattress was yellow with large circular stains all over it. In some spots, Dolly could recall blood being spilled, which caused the stains. The room was dark and quiet aside from the rolling thunder outside and a singular fan that ran nonstop, coursing air through the hairs that

stood on end all over Papa's ass crack.

Another new sense for Dolly was smell. The room smelled of something foul, perhaps from deep within someone.

A wet rumble could be heard coming from Papa. Dolly couldn't help but feel disgusted at the sound, but the smell that followed was nothing short of deadly.

She slowly climbed down off her shelf, stumbling when she first found her footing. Growing and using muscles are two completely different things.

Dolly slowly began to tip-toe toward the bed; the grumbling man still sounded asleep. Her face barely reached the side of the bed when he began to stir.

She froze, holding her breath.

If Papa wakes up, I'm done for.

He rolled over, his hairy testicles glistening in sweat between his legs. He opened them and scratched his balls before placing his hand under his nose and falling back asleep.

Dolly moved carefully, one foot in front of the other. Her dress swayed with her movements. At that moment, she knew she would need help.

The girl in the basement.

She tip-toed as fast as her little legs could carry her, making her way to the basement door, which luckily had been left open. She shimmied down each step before her eyes caught sight of Rebecca, still bound to the

metal frame of the old bed. She was naked, and blood remained smeared across her pubic mound. She was no older than thirteen, still with her budding nipples that hadn't fully formed amongst her breasts.

"Hello?" whispered Dolly.

Rebecca jumped, attempting to sit up where she lay but unable to fully erect herself.

"Who's there?" Rebecca wondered aloud. Fear was strewn across her face.

"Don't be scared and don't scream."

Dolly stepped off the bottom step, appearing in the soft glow of the overhead lightbulb that was held by a single wire.

"Are… are you a little girl?"

"No – actually, yes. I am. You're not the first girl he's doing this to, and you won't be the last. We've got to get you out of here."

Dolly hurried across the room and climbed into the bed. She hopped across Rebecca and untied each wrist, finally allowing her to sit up.

Rebecca rubbed her wrists and then looked down in between her legs.

"Oh my god…" she began to sob.

"It's okay. I know it's bad, but you're a strong girl, so we can get through this. But we need to take him out."

"What do you mean?" Rebecca asked. She continued to rub her wrists. Tears fell down her cheeks.

"We're going to need to get him to come back down here."

Rebecca shook her head violently.

"Please, no. I can't do that again. Please," she begged.

"Listen to me." Dolly straddled the sobbing girl and held her bruised cheeks in her tiny hands. "I won't let anything happen."

∞ ∞ ∞

With the two girls in place, Rebecca let out a blood-curdling scream.

"Ahhhhhh – help me!" she yelled as she kicked and fought against the ties that were now loosely hanging over her wrists. "Somebody help me! I've been kidnapped!"

Ruckus could be heard above their heads as Papa stumbled out of bed. The girls froze.

"Here he comes," whispered Dolly.

The large man waddled down the rickety wooden staircase.

"Shut the fuck up!" he yelled, making his way toward her. She continued screaming. As Papa approached the bed, Dolly quickly grabbed both of his ankles from underneath. Just as Papa's shocked gaze turned toward her, their eyes meeting for the first time ever, Rebecca arose from the mattress and lunged toward him, sending him toppling over backward. His head bounced with a loud thud upon impact, and he didn't move after.

"Is he dead?" asked Rebecca as she leaned over the edge of the mattress.

"No, he's just unconscious. Quick, grab those ties, and let's get him tied together."

For what seemed like ages, the

two girls worked tirelessly to move Papa from the floor to the blood-stained mattress and secure him to the bedposts.

"Now, we just wait for him to wake up."

"Dolly?" grumbled Papa as he slowly moved his head back and forth. "Why does my head hurt so bad? I could've sworn I saw Dollface for a minute."

"You did, you gigantic tub of lard."

"What the fuck! How did – how are you –," he cut himself off.

"Yeah, Papa. I'm alive and kickin'," she said, sashaying her hip out to the side.

"You look sexy as fuck."

"I'm a three-year-old!"

"Can I see it?"

"See what," replied Dolly.

"Let me see under your panties. Just once. Please." Papa heaved heavily as he spoke.

"Why? Why Papa? So you can do to me what you've done to all those girls all these years? You're disgusting. You're a fucking pig, and I'm going to make you regret everything you ever did to every single little girl. Rebecca, go get the supplies I told you about."

"Okay," she replied softly, now clothed in what she wore just earlier in the day.

As they waited for Rebecca's return, Dolly retrieved a rag from a corner of the table and laid it evenly

across Papa's face. She stood directly above him and removed her panties.

"What're you doing?" he asked from beneath the dirty rag, unable to see.

Dolly had never known what it was like to urinate before, but she felt the stinging welling up inside her, and she knew this was something that needed to be released.

"Remember that little girl – I think her name was Jenny. Remember Jenny, Papa?"

"Be more specific."

"You waterboarded her to death."

"Ah, her. Yes. I came inside you right as she was dying. It was amazing."

Dolly perched her tiny frame over Papa's face. With her legs spread, her lips parted, and urine began to trickle down onto the rag.

"What are you doing?" asked Papa once more.

Suddenly, a gush of yellow liquid came streaming from Dolly's exposed parts. She tilted her head back, moaning, as she felt the joy of relieving herself for the first time ever. Beneath her, the urine spread throughout the dish rag rapidly. With the golden liquid quickly filling his nostrils, Papa began to wretch and cough under the weighted, wet rag.

"Stop!" he yelled. "I can't breathe!"

Clenching herself off, Dolly let the remainder of her piss trickle down

before she shook the remnants off and pulled her panties back up.

Beneath the rag, Papa lay panting, gasping for clean, unscented air as Rebecca came down the stairs holding two sacks.

"Here ya go," she said, handing the bags off to Dolly.

"Now the fun begins," she said.

Chapter Three

"You hungry?" asked Dolly to her new victim. Glaring back at her, she noticed his face was still wet with her urine. Dolly chuckled to herself.

"We have some fruit if you'd like some."

"I'm going to fuck you in the ass so hard that you literally bleed to death from it."

"That's not nice, Papa."

"Fuck you," he replied.

Rebecca took the bowl of fruit and approached Papa.

"Open up," she said as she thumbed the blueberries. They had been sitting at the back of the fridge for likely weeks, as they were half-goo and half-pubic hair washed up from a geriatric shower drain.

Rebecca shut his nose so he would be forced to open his mouth. She'd set a blueberry on his tongue each time and cover his mouth. The moist texture, mixed with what felt like hair, coated his tongue, sending goosebumps down his arms as he tried desperately to swallow the piece of fruit.

Belch.

"Awe, you're done already," asked Dolly from a small chair in the corner. He used to sit her in it and let her watch while he would fucked his victims to death. She knew he meant what he said to her, but it wouldn't be his small cock that caused his victims to meet death. It's his crushing weight after he orgasms.

"Do you remember Heather?"

Papa stared at her. He never cared to learn their names, just their dislikes.

"You treated her like a pig, remember?"

"Oh, yeah," he laughed. "I remember her; how could I forget."

"Roll over," said Dolly, nearly cutting him off.

"What?"

"Roll over, or I will take a shit in your mouth right now."

Papa squirmed on the bed for some time before finally rolling over on his heavy stomach. With his arms still bound but now in a cross, his naked ass was exposed for Dolly to do as she pleased.

"Cherry syrup, please," Dolly asked Rebecca. Dollface was standing between Papa's bare legs. Rebecca handed her the glass bottle of cherry syrup.

She dabbed a bit on her finger before swirling it around her fingertips. Licking it off, she moaned aloud, "Mmmm, Papa. You'll like this one," she said before taking the squirt bottle and spreading his butt cheeks.

"It's sweet, just like your little baby girl."

With his hairy asshole exposed, it puckered in and out, awaiting something it didn't know it would receive.

Dolly placed her moist fingertip on his puckered ass, twirling it around his hair.

"You like your ass played with, Papa?" she asked.

"Mmmmmm, yessssss," he groaned into the mattress.

Dolly held his cheeks apart with her other hand as she reached for the cherry syrup. She slid the tip of the glass bottle against his asshole.

"Want me to go in, Papa?"

"Yessssss, fuck me," he groaned once more.

In a swift motion, she slammed the neck of the bottle into his virgin asshole. She could see through the clear glass that his sphincter was tightening around it. Papa let out a loud cry.

"Owwwwwwwwww!" he yelped, clenching his cheeks tightly in an attempt to push out the cold glass.

Dolly tilted the bottle further, letting the cherry syrup spill out into him.

"Your ass is gonna be delicious," she laughed. "Look at it go!" The bright red liquid was quickly being sucked deep inside him.

Gulp.

Gulp.

Gulp.

His asshole continued drinking the sugary mixture, holding it deep within him. However, the more that poured in, the more remnants of his insides washed back into the bottle. Small chunks of feces now floated in the main chamber of the glass container. Dolly tilted the bottle further, pressing the end of the neck into the bottom half of his rectum, sending shooting pains throughout his body as it slowly stretched him.

"Butt plug, please! Hurry!"

Rebecca appeared holding a Jupiter-sized plug with a pink gemstone end that was meant for the most professional of sex workers. Ripping the bottle out of his ass, she

quickly crammed the butt plug inside him, watching as his asshole spread to unthinkable width, sucking in the head of the plug before it disappeared completely, his sphincter eating away at it.

Dollface smacked his ass.

"How's that feel?"

Papa cried into the mattress.

"You used that same plug on a teenage girl, so I don't want to hear it."

"He really did all these things to other girls?" asked Rebecca. Her eyes told a story that no teenage girl should ever tell.

Dolly's face softened when looking at the poor girl.

"He did a lot of things to many

people, Rebecca. But this is *your* story of vindication. What's next?"

Rebecca smiled.

"Did he ever do anyone's fingernails?"

Chapter Four

Papa's fingers were outstretched on the wall, his wrists still tightly tethered to the rusted bed frame.

Leaning down into his ear, Dollface whispered, "This is for Lucy."

"Which one was Lucy?" Papa replied before being sent off into a screaming frenzy.

Dolly pressed the butter knife under Papa's dirty pinky nail. Slowly, she moved the knife further, wedging

the nail at an angle the further it went.

"Oh, God, please stop!" he cried out.

"What did you say to Lucy before you took off her nails? *If you're not hard, you're soft*? Was that it?"

"What the fuck are you talking about, you crazy bitch?!"

"Let's try hard," she said before suddenly ramming the knife completely under the pinky nail and sending it soaring past their heads. Papa screamed furiously while tears began to pour down his cheeks.

"How old was Lucy, do you remember?" she asked over the wailing. Dolly placed the knife under the pointer finger and forcefully wedged it off.

"Fuck you!" he sobbed.

"She was eleven years old."

Dolly repeated the same process with the next finger.

"Do you remember why you removed her fingernails?" she asked. Papa remained burdened by the cool air touching his exposed finger skin. All he could do was sob and spit saliva onto the dirty mattress. "You were upset that she had already gone through puberty."

"He removed an eleven-year-old's fingernails for that?" asked Rebecca, shocked.

Dolly nodded as she placed the next finger in her hand. She drove the knife under the fingernail with such force that the dull blade penetrated

the quick of the nail after it popped off.

"Owwwwwww," he cried out once more. "Please, Dolly, I'm begging you to stop. Please."

"Lucy begged too, Papa."

She held his thumb in place, driving the knife around its edges.

"Lucy repeatedly begged you to stop taking off her fingernails, and you wouldn't listen."

The blade slid slightly further under the thumbnail.

"When you anal raped her, and she couldn't even grip the bed because she had no fingernails left," she said callously as she plunged the knife further, wedging it with force to remove the nail slowly. "She begged and cried for you to stop, you fucking

dollop of dick curds," finished Dolly in her child-like voice.

Not feeling complete with herself, she reached up to her ear and removed the singular pearl earring. She held Papa's hand again and eyeballed his exposed thumb.

The ridges of where the nail used to be were discolored and peeling from the layers of skin that came off with it. Where the nail sat was a white color that appeared moist.

Dolly stabbed the earring into the pruney-like texture of the sensitive nail bed.

"FUUUUUCK you, bitch!" Papa screamed.

"I could do this all day!" she giggled.

"Poke. Poke. Poke," she laughed as she went to each finger one-by-one, poking at the flesh where Papa's fingernails used to be.

"If you're not hard, you're soft!" she cried out in glee, slamming the earring down onto his pinky, penetrating the sensitive flesh.

"Poke, again!" she cried out again, penetrating the next finger's flesh. She worked her way back and forth over each finger's most sensitive area, stabbing them relentlessly to ensure the most horrific pain.

"Rebecca, please be a doll and locate all the nails for me." Rebecca nodded before hopping out of her seat and scattering about the small room.

"What ..." sighed Papa. "Ahem. What ... are you gonna do?"

"Papa! Haven't you learned to just shut the fuck up by now? Asking questions gets you nowhere."

Rebecca gathered all five.

"Good. Now to start on the left hand." Papa cried.

∞ ∞ ∞

With all ten fingernails removed, Papa lay helplessly face down on the mattress, his bare ass exposing the tufts of hair that were growing in thick, black patches all over his back. Pustules had formed, including the one on his penis that had been there for months.

"If you so much as move a muscle during this process, I will slit your fucking throat, is that understood?" asked Dollface.

"Yes."

She walked across the bed and positioned herself in between his legs once more. With a forceful tug, she

removed the butt plug and watched small gushes of red liquid come with it.

One by one, she placed each fingernail in his asshole, their sharp edges scraping his insides along the way. Finally, she replaced the plug and walked back to his face.

"Clean me up," she said. Papa looked at her confused, then excitement shot across his face as he pondered the possibilities of what she meant.

"My hand, you perverted pignut." Dolly placed her child-like hand completely inside Papa's mouth as she rolled it around his tongue, making sure that he consumed every drop of cherry juice that had seeped from his bursting asshole.

Dolly popped a strawberry in her mouth as she smiled.

Chapter Five

Papa continued crying into the mattress. His fingertips felt like they were on fire, with small puncture holes all in them. He wondered to himself if it was truly that barbaric for the girls, but he couldn't let his mind wander too far down that path.

Not until he figured out a way out of the situation he somehow managed to get himself in.

Fucking bitches, he thought to

himself in between sobs. *They're going to get what's coming to them.*

"Whatcha doin' over there, Pops," asked Dollface from a darkened corner. She had been eyeing him for some time and wondered what was going through that balding head of his.

"Fuck off," he replied.

"Ya know, all this could stop if you just tell me to kill you, and I will." Dolly was met with silence. "Very well, then. Rebecca, can you get me the razor?"

Papa's head slowly sat up.

"Razor?"

"Nope. Too late, Papa. We are already moving on," replied Dolly.

"Wait! What're you doing with a razor?!" he exclaimed. He tried to watch her from his belly-flat position, but his head couldn't quite make the turn far enough. Papa wriggled back and forth to the sounds of the tiny footsteps getting closer to him. "What're you doing, Dolly?!"

Rebecca appeared holding a pink shaving razor in her hand. Papa would often shave the older girl's pussies if they had too much pubic hair because he wanted them to appear as young as humanly possible.

Dolly eyed the disgusting body that lay before her, every hair and pustule exposed to the humid air of the basement. The stench that radiated off his body was unlike any other. Dolly recalled time and time

again Papa complaining about how he hated bathing. He'd often go weeks without a shower, letting the virgin blood from each girl completely dry to his small pecker. He would lay in bed at night naked, flicking the flakes of crimson off with his thumb while violently inhaling the fumes that radiated from his warm, moist undercarriage. He loved it. He loved the stench, as it allowed him to relive those moments with each girl.

Dolly stood over his back. With the razor in her hand, she began shaving him. The dry metal dragged and catching against each black hair.

"You're shaving me?" he asked, shocked.

The blade slowly made elongated strokes, carrying tufts of

long, scraggly hairs with it. Dolly kept up the long strokes while letting the hair build up on it.

She noticed she was coming to her first destination across his skin. As she got closer and closer to the first pustule, she could see his muscles beginning to tense under the pressure of the blade.

Whoosh. Closer.

Another passing whoosh fills the air.

Closer.

The corner of the razor's head caught the pustule. Papa jumped.

"Please don't do that," he pleaded.

Whoosh.

The blade passed by the other side of the pustule.

Dolly positioned the razor at the top of Papa's back. With light pressure, she slowly dragged the blade down his skin before stopping at the pus-filled cyst. Slowly and lightly, she dragged the blade across the pustule. The small rectangular pieces of metal immediately grabbed the skin, peeling it back and exposing yellow liquid. Papa screamed.

Dolly picked up the razor and placed it back just above the pustule. Pressing down harder this time, she slowly dragged it back down once more, carrying more flesh with it. Flimsy layers of skin had built up on the blades, and yellow pus with hints of blood inside it created a thickened

layer preventing further shaving. She needed to clean it.

Dolly held the razor to Papa's face.

"Clean it with your tongue," she said.

"You're out of your mind!"

In her frustration, she snatched both of his cheeks in her hand and shoved the entire razor into his mouth, moving it furiously in and out, raping his mouth hole as hard as she could as she made sure to rub the filthy pink razor across his tongue.

She removed the razor as he began to gag, spewing blood.

"You look like a beached whale. Roll over."

Without hesitation and between sobs, Papa obliged. He groaned when attempting to straighten his arms, them having been locked in place in a crisscross pattern for hours now. They hurt. Everything hurt, but nothing was as strong as the seething anger that felt like fire rising inside him.

Dolly watched his shrunken penis flop about when he rolled over. The pustule on it clearly needing a release. She picked up the butter knife that was used for his fingernails, and with a loud smack, she slapped Papa's ball sack with the metal utensil.

"Owwww," he cringed, bringing his legs up.

Dolly slapped him again, harder.

"Stop it, you bitch!" he finally cried out.

"Or...." Said Dolly, letting the butter knife meet his scrotum once more.

"You'll..."

Smack.

"Do...."

Smack.

"What?!"

SMACK.

Papa brought his legs to his oversized belly in a futile attempt at shielding the sack. With the butt plug exposed momentarily, Dolly grabbed the knife and began smacking it as he adjusted himself.

"Mmmm, fingernail cherry

ass."

SMACK.

The metal knife collided with the silicone toy.

With quick motions, Dolly placed the flaccid cock in her tiny hand while grabbing the razor simultaneously. She slid it down the side of his penis, letting the razor blades nick the wrinkled, crusty skin beneath it. Papa writhed in agony as droplets of blood flowed freely down his withered shaft.

In another elongated motion, she slid the blades down the head of the pustule, applying excessive pressure once she knew the razors were on the cyst.

Pop.

Yellow pus oozed from the head of the pustule as she scraped the razor blades repeatedly against it, pulling off elongated noodles of thinned skin.

"Spaghetti-skin dick?" she inquired. Papa continued to howl, kicking his legs in the hopes of dismantling the little girl from between them.

"I'm gonna fuckin' kill you!"

"Not if I kill you first, Mr. Pig Fucker!" she replied, continuing the back-and-forth motion on his bloody cock, pulling threads of skin. She took the skin and placed it delicately in her hand.

"Hungry?!" she asked as she shoved her small fist into Papa's bloody mouth, forcing his cock skin down his throat before removing her

hand quickly and covering his mouth.

Papa continued to gag on the flesh of his own penis, fighting violently against the small girl that had him in a vice. He couldn't withstand any more torture, pus, or flesh. The thought of what was sliding down his throat made his stomach churn, sending leftover food from the night before coursing upwards through his body. Finding his throat, he wretched against Dolly's hands covering him. Chunks of vomit quickly filled his mouth as it mixed with the bits of dick skin that he had yet to swallow.

"Pfuh-leeeeze" he cried out from beneath her hand. The vomit had nowhere to go. He swallowed, forcing bits of his genitals down into his

stomach along with the chunks of acidic dinner.

"Good boy," said Dolly, patting his cheek. "I didn't know you swallowed."

Chapter Six

Rebecca had curled up on a blanket on the floor as she watched the main attraction events take place.

"Do you know when I can go home?" she said softly.

"Oh, yeah, honey. Soon, I promise."

"Did he do all that, too?"

"Do what?" replied Dolly, glancing at the young girl.

"The vomit."

"Oh, yes."

"How?"

"You sure you want to know?" Rebecca nodded. "There was a little girl named Karen many years ago. She was around your age. Papa put his cock in her throat and kept it there. She vomited on it, over and over, until eventually she suffocated."

Rebecca grimaced before looking away. "What a scumbag," she whispered to herself.

"But the orgasm was amazing," said Papa.

Dolly slapped him across the face. "Shut the fuck up, no one asked you."

Papa sat up as quickly as possible, twisting his left wrist repeatedly before jerking his arm as hard as he could. He knew it would hurt his wrist; he'd been preparing for this moment in his head for some time now. Yes, he *could* withstand the wrist pain, but there was no way he could continue the torture.

With a quick flick, his wrist broke free. Dollface gasped before she realized she was being struck across the face and sent soaring off the bed. She landed on her back on the floor.

Papa leaped from the bed, ripping his other wrist from the tie with such force that it left an indentation across his skin.

Dolly scrambled to her feet.

"Not so fast, bitch!" he said,

catching a wad of her coconut hair in his grasp. She screamed, kicking at him. Papa grabbed her ankles and ripped them back from under her feet, landing her on her back on the concrete floor. He pulled her to him as she continued screaming.

"Help me," she yelled toward Rebecca who was frozen in place, unable to move in fear that she would be a distraction and Papa would come for her again. "Please!"

Papa rose to his knees and spread Doll's legs apart. Rebecca watched in abject terror as her captor began to violate Dolly. Her eyes froze on the movements in front of her as if she were a small, doe-eyed fawn meeting the hunter for the first time.

Doll's pink gaze glistened under

the hue of the yellow overhead lamp. It looked as though she wanted to cry, and for a split second, Rebecca thought she might.

The two girls locked eyes.

It was as if, at that moment, they shared something special. Something traumatizing but something unforgettable.

Rebecca slowly began to rise to her feet. Glancing quickly around the room, she needed an object to take Papa out. Dolly continued to kick and scream just enough to keep him distracted so Rebecca could move around freely.

She slinked around the table and eyed the golf clubs that were sitting under the stairs. She could feel her bare toes sticking to the concrete

floor as she began to tip-toe across the room, moving with grace as if the wind were carrying her.

She made her way behind Papa, feeling Dolly's eyes on her. Retrieving a club, Rebecca firmly held it in both hands as she steadily moved back toward Papa.

She raised the heavy club over her head, feeling the weight from it weighing her arms down above her head. With a quick sigh, she swung the club through the air as hard as she could.

Papa's head fell with a loud thud, and he collapsed onto Dollface.

She froze in time. Her babyish eyes wanted to cry, but she knew she had to be strong. With Papa collapsed on top of her, Dolly took a moment to

consider her next move.

"Help," she asked through a muffled voice. Rebecca mustered all her strength to begin rolling Papa off Dolly.

"Are you okay?" asked Rebecca.

"I'll be fine," replied Dolly. She sat up and adjusted her dress. The stench of copper permeated her tiny nostrils. "I have an idea."

∞ ∞ ∞

apa had been draped over the side of the bed while sitting on his knees. His right arm was extended and held to the post at the top of the bed with thick ropes. The left arm was extended, as well, to the bottom of the bed.

The wound on the back of his head placed a small dent in his cranium, surrounded by blood that had dried to his dirty hair.

The end of a shop vacuum tube had been placed in his mouth, and the edges were held to his lips with super glue.

Papa stirred.

"Mmmm. Hmmm, mmmmmmmm," he groaned, his voice echoing through the end of the tube.

"Morning sunshine," said Dollface as she walked around the bed while standing over him. The blood, having dried in between her legs, was beginning to itch.

"Mmmmmmmmm," he cried out, realizing the current situation.

"What's the worst thing you've ever eaten, Papa?" asked Dolly, her legs still trembling beneath her. Papa continued to groan into the end of the tube. His eyes were as wide as they would go as fear cascaded across his face.

Dolly poured another bottle of cherry juice down the tube and

watched as it hit Papa's open throat. He gagged at the sugary mixture, his eyes filling with tears as he tried to keep them open. Snot trailed from his nose while a cacophony of gagging and guttural sounds exited the end of the tube.

Placing a strawberry on her tongue, she tossed the glass bottle across the room.

"Listen up, beef-slug. I have a proposition for you."

Papa's eyes darted toward Dolly, watching her pace back and forth across the room.

"If you let me cut off your balls, I'll let you go. But you must eat them. If you don't, I'm afraid you'll eat something else soon."

Papa sobbed into the tube. He knew deep within the back of his fucked-up mind that whatever was coming next would, without a doubt, likely be the worst moment of his entire life. His cock throbbed as if it had been thrust into the depths of hell. His stomach ached. His asshole burned. His fingertips stung. There wasn't a piece of him that didn't hurt in some way, and he knew it was about to get significantly worse.

Papa weighed his options. Was she going to kill him? His eyes darted back and forth across the room. Everything was blurry behind the tears, but he could make out Dolly's movements as she continued pacing the room around him, eating her strawberries.

He had made his decision.

"Mmmmmm   mmmm mmmmm," he said into the tube.

Dolly paused.

"What was that?" she asked.

Papa turned frantic. "Mmmmm mmmmm mmm mmmm!"

"Sorry, I can't quite understand you. One more time?"

Papa closed his eyes in frustration before letting out a guttural scream through the tubing. Dolly could sense the fear in his voice.

She giggled as she picked up the end of the tubing, stretching it along the floor.

Chapter Seven

Dolly's tongue wriggled inside her mouth. She enjoyed the feeling of food. Something she had always seen happening in front of her but could never experience. Strawberries were her favorite of everything she had tried so far. The moist innards of these beautiful, little red berries had Dollface's tummy in a tizzy. She couldn't get enough of them. One by one, she plopped them on her tongue

and chewed, bursting sweet juice all over her mouth before swallowing.

If only Papa had introduced her to foods sooner, then maybe she would know what was best for the palate.

Dolly ran the tube alongside Papa, with the end resting just below his pulsating ball sack in between his legs. The butt plug was still deep within his asshole, holding in the cherry juice and fingernails. Dolly tapped the plug.

"How's that feel, my little milksop," she asked. Papa writhed at the tapping, feeling the juices welling inside his anal cavity.

Dolly placed her small hand over the butt plug, wrapping her tiny fingers around its edges. She found them buried within the tapestry of

Papa's thick asshole hair, littered with dingleberries and remnants of sticky, red sugar.

Craning her neck to the side, she gave the plug a slight tug. Watching closely so as not to spill out any internal contents, she admired the way Papa's sphincter loosened around the bulb before tightening again on the tip of the plug. Papa's back arched as it exited his body, his virgin asshole pulsating upon the release as cherry juice caught in the ass hairs.

Dolly positioned the end of the tube up against the lower half of his buttocks, angling it upwards to ensure every drop of cherry innards was savored. Once the tubing was in place, Rebecca began wrapping it in duct tape.

Dolly swiped her hands together before taking a seat on the mattress in front of Papa's face.

"Hungry?" she asked. He closed his eyes, doing everything he could not to release any of the butt juices into the tube. He could already taste the fumes of his unclean hole on his taste buds, which made him want to vomit, but he knew that vomiting would essentially be the death of him. Every scenario played out callously through his mind. Should he shit and swallow? Get it over with? Go little by little? Hold it in as long as possible in an attempt to wait them out? He had many options, but none of the options resulted in him walking out of there without feces stuck in his teeth. Papa's fire continued to rage inside him as tears streamed down his cheeks. He

wanted to kill her.

Rebecca approached from the side.

"I wanna go home," she said.

"I know. You will soon," said Dollface.

"No. I wanna go home – now!" she yelled, launching her foot forward, sending it directly into Papa's stomach. He lurched forward as the sound of liquid erupted throughout the tube.

Papa groaned as he unwillingly pushed harder, feeling the automatic release as cherry juice shot out of his asshole and into the tube. With his stomach in a knot, the pain caused him to push more as he felt chunks of shit exit his asshole. He could feel the

nails scraping down each side of his anus, ripping the tender flesh inside him as the blood mixed with the shit-infested cherry juice.

"Here we go," said Dolly, placing another strawberry on her tongue.

Like a flowing river, the juice shot its way through the tube, carrying blood, fingernails, and broken pieces of his own shit with it. The chunks of fecal matter slammed into the side of the tubing as it was forcefully ejected from Papa's ass, sending it all barricading around the first corner of the tube and down toward Papa's face. His eyes closed before the first bit of cherry juice found his throat sending his eyes shooting open.

Little by little, Papa screamed

louder, his eyes rolling into the back of his head as he tried to keep his throat open to prevent himself from choking on his own shit.

Tears continued to pour down his face. Without warning, Papa felt his stomach churn, and his throat began to constrict, sending vomit-infused shit cherry juice back up into the tube. Papa's tongue danced around freely in the juices as drool pooled on the mattress beneath him.

Dolly and Rebecca watched in silence as their captor fought against his own body. Rebecca unwrapped the tape from Papa's rear and approached his face, holding the tubing high above her head.

"Good girl," said Dollface, smiling on.

The tube collected every drop of juice, shit, bile, and vomit built up in Papa's mouth as it was held up. His body lurched forward in waves as he shut his eyes and began swallowing.

Gulp.

Gulp.

Gulp.

Little by little, every bit of Papa went right back inside him.

Dolly leaned forward, placing her face next to his.

"I'm impressed. You have the gall to withstand more than I had originally given you credit for," she said as she placed the last strawberry in her mouth.

Small beads of sweat trickled

down his forehead.

"The better news is that everything you just swallowed will have more time to ferment before it comes out of you again."

Papa closed his eyes. He couldn't go through that again. The anger that burned within him slowly dissipated in his fight for survival. He wanted nothing more than to be able to sleep. He would never touch another girl again if Dolly would just let him go, but he couldn't tell her that. He couldn't tell her anything with the fucking tube in his mouth. He just wanted to be let go.

Dolly slid off the bed and walked to Rebecca.

Looking up at her, she asked, "What would you like to do next?"

"I want to go home," Rebecca replied. Her fight was also over. She had gotten her revenge, and at this point, she didn't care whether he lived or died; she just wanted to see her parents again.

"Agreed. Do the honors?" asked Dolly as she picked up a serrated knife from the bag of tools. Looking up at Rebecca, she smiled and handed it to her.

Papa tried to see what was happening. His eyes were wide and full of fear. Suddenly, pain forced its way, soaring through his entire body. His pores opened like small barrels of guns as sweat immediately began to pour from his glands. Everything all over burned as the tugging continued until it stopped.

"This one's for me," said Rebecca.

He watched her place something in the tube before holding it up over her head.

The objects rolled down the tubing and landed right on Papa's tongue.

His balls.

He was about to eat his own balls.

Frantic from the pain and the realization, his tongue flicked in a furious frenzy as it attempted to get the nut-sack off it, which sent it rolling toward Papa's throat.

His eyes widened further.

They were stuck.

He couldn't breathe.

Papa's throat constricted as he tried to cough up his balls. Beginning to feel lightheaded from the loss of blood from his groin, Papa closed his eyes and attempted to swallow.

Nothing.

He tried gasping for air. They wouldn't move. As his breathing became more frantic, the air was unable to enter or exit his lungs. He didn't know what to do. Papa glanced around the room in a panic. This couldn't be it for him. He couldn't die this way, not after everything that had happened to him. He was in too much pain. He couldn't die like this, he thought.

He could feel life slipping away from him, but the only sounds he

could make out were the laughs from those two stupid *bitches*.

"Fucking freak!" cackled Rebecca, hocking a loogie directly into Papa's eyes. He tried to blink, but he was too tired.

With a wave of fatigue surrounding his body like a warm blanket, Papa closed his eyes and relaxed, letting his head fall forward.

"Dolly?" called Rebecca. "Dolly! No!"

Chapter Eight

Rebecca sat in the rocking chair in the living room as she heard sirens in the distance. The storm had finally cleared, and blue skies had opened to a beautiful sunrise.

The house was disgusting. This was the first time she had truly been able to examine everything, and she wondered why no one had suspected Papa of anything sooner.

Rebecca walked around the

room as trinkets from small girls decorated nicknacks all over the home. The orange carpet was stained in random red spots. The furniture smelled of sweaty testicles. Everything was hot, humid, stinky, and she knew she couldn't leave Dollface here.

"You're going to come with me," Rebecca said to Dolly, who sat in her silicone skin on Rebecca's hip.

The moment Papa succumbed to death, Dolly fell to the floor, losing all remnants of ever being human. Her pink eyes glistened above her luscious little doll face and lips, which curved into a slight smile.

The sirens were getting louder now, and Rebecca knew they would never believe she took down her

captor alone. She walked to the window as a slew of police cruisers and media vans surrounded the house. Rebecca suddenly felt a sense of security and ease.

A sinister smile crept across her face under the glow of the red and blue lights.

"Looks like we have more work to do," she whispered.

Books By
This Author

Madness In Tandem

TRIGGER WARNINGS: This book contains graphic violence, gore, sex, vomit, and other acts that some may deem offensive. Reader discretion is advised. This book has an optional playlist on Spotify titled Madness in Tandem by RJ Powell.

Adam and Tilly, a recently married

couple, vacation to a peaceful cabin situated by a serene lake to spend a week of relaxation. The trip offers Tilly a chance to work on her latest book while enjoying the tranquillity. However, their plans are disrupted by a series of strange events that occur shortly after their arrival.

Eight Cases Of Jane

Warning to the reader: this

document contains acts that some may deem offensive, including cannibalism, torture, gore, Satanism, biblical references, outdated medical terminology, inflammatory LGBTQIA + subject matter, and more.

Jane Murphy killed eight men between the dates of October 1995 and January 1996. This is Jane's psychiatric interview.

Printed in Dunstable, United Kingdom